Aft̲̲̲̲̲̲̲̲̲̲̲̲̲̲̲̲̲̲̲̲̲

and

Fool Me Once

AMY LAURENS

OTHER WORKS

Find more works by the author at
www.amylaurens.com

Aftermath & Fool Me Once

INKLET #57

AMY LAURENS

Inkprint PRESS

www.inkprintpress.com

Print ISBN: 978-1-925825-59-6
eBook ISBN: 9781393974789

www.inkprintpress.com

National Library of Australia Cataloguing-in-Publication Data
Laurens, Amy 1985 –
Aftermath and Fool Me Once (Double Issue)
46 p.
ISBN: 978-1-925825-59-6
Inkprint Press, Canberra, Australia
1. Fiction—Fantasy—Paranormal 2. Fiction—Fantasy—Urban 3. Fiction—Horror 4. Fiction—Short Stories

First Print Edition: May 2021
Cover design © Inkprint Press
Interior art © Amy Laurens

AFTERMATH

"Are you alright?"

I snorted. "Oh, yes. Absolutely."

Cran gave me a sidelong look. "I was only asking."

"And I was only answering." I shifted so's he couldn't see my face, and stared out the window. "Of course I'm fine. Why wouldn't I be? It was only a small demon, teeny tiny. Barely worth exorcising." My jaw twitched as I tried to hold back the sarcasm.

Silence for a moment, then I heard the rustle of cloth as he stood.

He left without saying a word.

I was glad.

I waited a while to be sure he wasn't coming back, then I went to the sideboard and poured myself a few too many finger-heights of lemon vodka. I glanced away so I didn't have to see my hands tremble.

I was fine. The demon was gone. It had needed barely any prompting, even; just a splash of holy water, a garlic sandwich and a quick prayer— gone.

A tiny demon.

Insignificant.

So why did I feel so damn messed up?

I gulped down the alcohol, ignoring the burn in my throat, and slumped back down on the lounge. I stared out the window, smiling half-heartedly as Molly-the-insane-labradoodle chased the neighbour's cat across the lawn.

Yesterday, if someone'd told me what was going to happen, I'd've called *them* insane. Actually, I'd've prob'ly called them a bloody idiot, get out of my way now, thanks very much. But whatever.

I closed my eyes and draped a hand over my face. The sunlight seemed extra bright and shiny today, and it hurt my eyes to look outside for long.

Something moved behind me and I jumped, whipping out the crucifix from down my shirt. "Dammit, Cran," I said. "Did you have to come in so suddenly like that?"

He looked abashed. "Sorry."

Cran never said sorry. My grip on the crucifix tightened and I found myself wishing I could switch my alco for water—the holy kind. "What did you say?"

He glanced up at me. "I said sorry. I know you're pretty jumpy still. I'll try to make more noise."

He tried on a grin.

I narrowed my eyes. Was it just that my recent freak-out had put me on edge, or did something about him seem different to normal? A tightness around the eyes, a twitch of the lips, something in the carriage of his shoulders...

The crucifix dug into my palm. I set the drink down and shoved my hand into my pocket, looking for the last stray clove of garlic. It came up empty. Hell.

I edged towards the kitchen. "So, uh, big plans for today?" I asked.

Cran shrugged. "Game's on tonight, I was thinking of heading over to Mickey's to watch."

"Oh, yeah?" I said with deliberate casualness. The demon was good, very good. I could almost believe I was just making the whole thing up. If it hadn't just possessed me yesterday, if I hadn't seen its tics and mannerisms up close and personal, I'd've missed the whole exchange going on on Cran's face: demon versus man, the internal struggle for control.

"Yeah," the demon said with Cran's voice. "You?"

I stuck my bottom lip out nonchalantly. "Nothing much. Still, you know." I held up my free hand and stared at it, transfixed for a second by the shaking. *Bastard*, I thought. *You did this to me and you know it. I'll kill you this time. What was it that killed demons for good, again?*

Cran gave me a sympathetic look. "Yeah. That. Not much fun, I reckon."

I shrugged and made it to the kitchen, sliding in behind the bench and pretending I was rummaging for something to eat. "I lived," I said.

You won't, I added in the privacy of my own skull—which, thank God, was private once again.

Bastard demon. First me, now Cran.

It wasn't going to get away with this.

Stakes, that was it. Like vampires, their cousins. One big happy life-stealing family. I ground my teeth.

Cran moved toward me. "So how long do you think it will take? To, you know, recover?"

I fished around in the utensil drawer for the big bamboo chopsticks. A stick was nearly a stake, right? Near enough was good enough, or at least I bloody well hoped it would be. "No idea," I told Cran. "S'pose it depends."

"Yeah?" He—the demon—responded. "On what?"

I shrugged again. "Things."

"Can I help?"

Hell, he was right behind me. I could feel him breathing down my neck. I shivered. "Yeah," I said. "Yeah, you can."

He put his hands on my shoulders. "How?" His mouth was right next to my ear. His breath was warm.

Bastard. Why Cran? Why the only man who'd ever loved me in my entire miserable life? Bloody, bloody hell. "Like this," I whispered.

I twisted around, one clean movement, too quick for him to react. The crucifix slammed into his forehead, the bamboo stake into the side of his neck.

His eyes went wide. "What the—"

He gurgled.

I pushed him off me and he crumpled to the floor, and I tried to pretend I wasn't crying. "You bastard," I said through the tightness in my throat. "I name you Azazel."

The air shimmered in front of me. "You rang?"

I blinked, regained my senses.

Scrambled backwards. "What the *hell*?"

The faint outline of the demon lifted an eyebrow. "You called. I appeared,

13

despite the *warmth* of your reaction last time. To what do I owe the honour this time?"

My gaze flickered between the hazy demon, hovering in the middle of the kitchen, and the crumpled, broken body lying beneath it. "You possessed him. You bastard, you possessed the only man I ever loved!"

The demon glanced down. "That hunk of meat? Hardly. So few brain cells it would be like ingesting water to stave off famine. And the few that he has—had—were far too good to be pleasant." It shuddered. "No, thank you. I have better taste than that."

I stared. "No. You possessed him. I saw you!"

The demon huffed. "If you think, even for a *second*, that I would possess something like *that*..." It trailed off, head tilted, staring at the bamboo skewer in my hand.

I followed its gaze and stared horrified as the blood trickled down to meet my fingers.

"Oh, you didn't. You didn't!" The demon cackled. "Oh, my precious, that is just *too* lovely." It cackled louder. "Well done!"

I drew in a shaky breath. "Get lost," I said.

It clutched its sides, laughing uproariously.

"Now," I said, anger hardening in my chest. I stood, took aim, threw the stake and the crucifix all at once.

The laughter cut off. The shimmer snapped out with a shriek.

I stared at the body lying glassy-eyed on the floor. The demon was gone.

So was Cran.

THE MAKING OF
AFTERMATH

I'll be honest, I don't have an interesting backstory for this story, largely because it arrived fully formed.

It was around the time I was learning to write short stories by doing a weekly short story challenge with friends, pre-2010 at some point. I needed a story, and this one was literally just *there*.

What if the demon-hunter made a mistake? What if, because of paranoia and probable-PTSD they started seeing signs of possession in everyone, possessed or not?

What if, what if, what if...

FOOL ME ONCE

Larelle sank into her armchair by the fire, cosy and pleasantly drowsy. The comforting scent of woodsmoke wound around her, and she sighed. The kids had been a riot today; she was smashed. Even sitting upright was too much effort, and she slumped against the padded innards of the chair, wondering if curling her legs up under her would be worth the effort/comfort trade off. Thank heavens it was Friday.

A knock sounded at her apartment door and, staring into the flickering blue-orange flames and glowing embers, Larelle called out, "Come in!"

The door creaked open. Larelle waited for Jason's footsteps, but they didn't come.

"You're early," she said, pivoting around to the door, thoughts full of languid disappointment that she had not had time to change.

Her heart skipped, then double-pounded. The figure smiling toothily on the near side of the threshold was not Jason.

Partially because Jason wasn't six-foot-three with long, dark hair and muscles like something out of a firemen's calendar—but mainly because Jason couldn't leer at her with jet black eyes—sclera included—and pointed, gleaming fangs.

"Actually," the vampire-apparent said, "I believe I'm exactly on time. I do like to eat dessert before my mains. Bad habit, I know."

"Better for the digestive system," Larelle said reflexively; her Year 3 students had been studying the systems of the human body this month.

Not that she'd told them the bit about dessert first, of course. She wanted permanency, not a civil lawsuit from parents. "And can't you only enter houses when invited?"

"True," said the vampire, and he licked his fangs. "And it was so *sweet* of you to invite me in." He rubbed his hands gleefully. "Shall we begin?"

Larelle's chest constricted and her fingers tightened around each other in her lap as the fatal words played through her mind: Come in.

Idiot. She'd even had a peephole installed in the door right after that werewolf had attacked old Mrs Franklin, but did she bother to use it? No. Too much effort.

The fire crackled its critique of her work ethics, the pine she'd thrown on to get the blaze going fast snapping and popping.

Well, you know what else is a lot of effort? Larelle asked herself scathingly as she stood and paced towards the vampire. *Staking predators. Next time, just use the bloody peephole.* She grinned toothily, revealing the flecks of iron in her teeth—fillings she'd had done specially.

The vamp's cocksure smile slipped a little before he covered it with a grin even wider than hers—*Too wide,* she thought. *He's covering.*

"Oh yes," Larelle said, raising the iron-and-hardwood-and-silver poker from the fireplace—the ultimate multipurpose weapon against the supernatural. "Do let's begin."

The vampire lunged, but Larelle had done more than the basic training required by the government. She went down on one knee.

He grabbed over her head.

She stabbed the poker upward.

He died a fast, gurgling death.

She hoped it was painful.

Someone knocked at the door. Probably this was now Jason, but Larelle pulled the poker from the vampire's chest with a wet *schlurp*, wiped the vampire's copper-scented, pale-blue blood off on his shirt, and headed to the peephole to make sure.

She wasn't making that mistake again.

THE MAKING OF
FOOL ME ONCE

This was a quick little piece that basically arrived fully formed, and in doing so, gave me a bit of a revelation about myself. I wrote this for the *Darkness & Good* blog back in early 2017, and as you'll have noted, the story starts with the protagonist making a mistake that is, really, a bit stupid.

She should have known better.

What happens next in my previous stories is SUDDEN, INESCAPABLE DEATH.

But this time, I realised that was how the story was going to go… and I decided to change it. Because it made me realise: I'm really, really *bad* at giving myself permission to make mistakes. It's a Thing I'm Working On, but certainly early-2017-me was still only just coming to grips with this realisation—partly from looking back over so much of the short stories I had written in my 20s, which were—when viewed through one lens—all about punishing naivety.

So this time, I decided to have the protagonist win. This time, she got hit by a mistake—a mistake she really should have known how to avoid, which is apparently, according to my subconscious conditioning, The Worst Kind Of Mistake—and she lived.

Not only did she *live*, she came back swinging, and *triumphed* in the end.

Because, let's face it, that's how life mostly goes.

Maybe not always the triumphing bit, but we're all human, we all make mistakes, and if we let ourselves flounder after every single one, we'd be nothing but a ball of mush hiding under the blankets stinking of fear and self-loathing.

Been there. Done that. Not interested in a repeat.

So here's to our protagonist. May she live on as a reminder to us all that, fallible and stupid though we may sometimes be, in the end, we can still hit back at life—and win.

Read more by Amy Laurens!

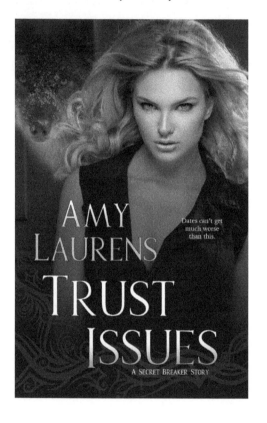

TRUST ISSUES

WARM STEAM FILLED THE AIR AROUND Becca, faintly scented with fake apples from her shampoo. The hot water pattered down on her back, turning her skin red and, in theory, soothing away her tension. Of course, that would have been more easily facilitated had she not been in the midst of performing the contortions necessary to get her legs shaved, but she'd feel better once she was done. Probably.

Up, rinse, up, rinse; she scraped the blossom-pink razor over her pale legs, shaking it out in the main stream of the shower water at the top of each stroke. Steam billowed up in her face as she curled over her leg, warm against her cheeks and the inside of her nose.

There. Nearly done.

Honestly, the whole thing was an exercise in pointless futility. It wasn't like the wolf was going to be staring at her legs. And if he did, so what? Why did she care what he thought?

She didn't, that's what. Jaw clenching, Becca pressed shower water from her eye with the tips of her fingers.

One last stroke.

Becca inhaled sharply as the razor sliced the sensitive skin over her Achilles heel, removing a good slice of flesh and making the water run momentarily red.

She grabbed at her ankle with her free hand, trying to stem the bleeding with her thumb, and nearly slipped on the wet tiles. Her elbow smacked the bottles of hair products that lined the shower's shelf—and the shelf itself—and she hopped madly, trying to regain her balance. Her weight fell against the cold glass of the shower screen—and the door screaked open, dumping her unceremoniously on the mat.

"Ow." That was going to bruise her butt.

Disgusted, Becca threw the razor back into the shower and scrambled to her feet. She reached in and turned the water off, realising as she did that her right elbow was about as tender as her butt would be in the morning. She flung her dark blonde, wet hair out of her eyes. So much for getting pretty.

Stupid date.

Stupid wolf.

Red streaks on the mat caught her eye as she snagged her white towel off the rail: her heel, still dripping blood.

Bloody hell.

Literally.

She gathered her wet hair to one side, picking it off her shoulders and neck, wrapped the towel around herself, and hobbled to the vanity. Somewhere in there, lost amid cobwebbed piles of lotions, powders and unused potions, was a packet of bandaids.

Becca crouched awkwardly, stretching into the back of the cupboard that stank of bleach and toothpaste—and jumped as her sore elbow connected with something cold: a festering bottle of nail polish that was only too happy to jump off the shelf and smash on the floor, bleeding its awful browny-coral innards all over the second bath mat.

The chemical scent of the polish hit her nostrils. *Urgh. Someone remind me why I am doing this?*

Perching on the edge of the bath, Becca applied the bandaid, a giant strip wider than two of her fingers, its 'flesh' tones doing nothing to blend in with the complexion her grandmother had liked to call porcelain. "Bloody Irish," she muttered.

She smoothed the plaster down, snatched up the bloodied bathmat and took it to the laundry, then stalked back to her room to dress.

Underwear, now that was a question. Not that there was any *question* of him *seeing* her underwear. She was widowed, not desperate. Even if, just occasionally, when he turned his big stupid wolf eyes on her she lost her mind just a little bit remembering what sex had been like.

But back to the underwear, she reminded herself as she finished towelling off and used the damp towel to twist up her hair. She didn't trust him as far as she could throw him, which given she doubted she could even lift him off the ground amounted practically to not at all—but could she really bring herself to go plain black cotton on a date?

Ah, screw it. It wasn't like the dress was that fitted or anything. Comfy it was. Becca fished her favourite pair of black undies out from the crumpled mess in her top drawer, donned a sensible—if slightly uplifting—bra, and from the very back of her other top drawer snatched out an old, dusty satin pencil case, the magenta one with the floral embroidery.

Despite nearly stabbing herself in the eye with mascara she hadn't applied in years, and overdoing it with the big round hairbrush and the hairdryer so it looked like she was wearing a 1960s wig for a few minutes until she managed to de-volumise things a bit, Becca managed to finish getting ready with a relative minimum of fuss.

She slipped into her little black dress—always go with a classic on the first date, she'd decided; she still wasn't actually sure whether she wanted to impress the wolf or scare him away—slipped her phone, driver's licence and bank card into the cunningly placed pocket, straightened the short sleeves, and squished into a pair of heels that were dangerously tall and stunningly gorgeous: black satin with red and gold oriental designs brocaded into the fabric, nearly six inches high.

She wobbled for the first few steps before remembering how to balance right in them: Weight on the toes, pretend the shoes aren't really there, just tip-toe along with your calves tight and your core strong.

You got this.

She caught sight of her reflection in her dresser mirror and sighed, confidence deflating. It had been so long since she'd done this. She'd been married to that two-faced jerk Nick for nearly three years, but they'd dated for another four or five before that.

She hadn't first-dated since she was what, eighteen? Nineteen?

Becca ran a hand over her forehead and exhaled. Nick was gone now. He might have stolen eight years of her life and literally any chance she ever had at having children of her own—the familiar flutter of regret and longing trembled through her stomach—but he was gone.

And the wolf was safe, at least inasmuch as he wouldn't lie to her upfront like Nick had.

Probably.

Maybe.

She hoped.

Really, there was no way to know. And trust wasn't exactly her specialty, when she was used to being able to detect lies and secrets right there in the head of anybody around her.

Urgh. Why, why am I doing this? This is such a bad idea.

As if on cue, her phone buzzed.

A message from her sister Clare: *I know he's picking you up in fifteen minutes, which means you're moping around wondering why you let me bully you into this, so I'm reminding you of our little bargain.*

Besides. He's gorgeous. It'll be good for you.

Becca's lips quirked to a half smile. Her sister knew her all too well—hence the bargain, whereby Becca would be subjected to an endless stream of potential suitors every time she visited Clare if she didn't agree to a date with the wolf. And simply avoiding Clare's house wouldn't have worked; Clare would have just hauled the suitors to her.

A knock sounded at the door.

Adrenalin leapt through Becca's stomach and she bolted upright, stuffing her phone back into her pocket, then heading to the door.

"I'm sorry," Wolf-boy said as she opened it. "I know it's not fashionable to be early, but the traffic was better than I'd planned."

He'd left his longish hair down, a perfectly-styled tangle of honey-brown waves that screamed to be touched, and although he was wearing a dark suit, he'd left his baby-blue shirt open at the neck, and the combination did little to hide the sheer breadth and power of his shoulders.

His golden eyes drilled through her, soft and amused and completely, utterly focused on her.

Becca realised she was staring and closed her mouth, working the inside of her lower lip between her teeth.

So the wolf scrubbed up well. That changed nothing. She'd known since she'd met him that he was sex-on-legs. That, she'd learned the hard way, was not even *close* to the top ten most important things in a relationship. "It's okay," she said. "I'm ready."

She stepped out the door, forcing him to step aside for her, and locked up the house. "Ready?" The smile she gave him was too bright, brittle like it might crack any moment, and she tried to relax.

He studied her carefully for just an instant too long, but nodded. "Sure, let's go."

Keep reading! Head to
www.inkprintpress.com/amylaurens/
secretbreaker/trustissues/
to buy your copy now!

ABOUT THE AUTHOR

AMY LAURENS is an Australian author of fantasy fiction for all ages. She has written the award-winning portal-fantasy *Sanctuary* series about Edge, a 13-year-old girl forced to move to a small country town because of witness protection (the first book is *Where Shadows Rise*), the humorous fantasy *Kaditeos* series, following newly graduated Evil Overlord Mercury as she attempts to acquire a castle, the young adult series *Storm Foxes*, about love and magic and family in small town Australia, and a whole host of non-fiction.

INKLETS

Collect them all! Released on the 1st and 15th of each month.

Allure
AMY LAURENS
INKLET #055

The LIES We KNOW
LIANA BROOKS
INKLET #056

DOUBLE
AFTERMATH & Fool Me Once
AMY LAURENS
INKLET #057

Purity
An Age Of Unicorns Story
AMY LAURENS
INKLET #058

Saved
AMY LAURENS
INKLET #059

A Kiss is the Secret
AMY LAURENS
INKLET #060

A Changing Tides Story
Fire Bright
AMY LAURENS
INKLET #061

Hades AND Persephone
LIANA BROOKS
INKLET #062

Just So Long As You're Happy
AMY LAURENS
INKLET #063

INKLET #064

Theft Of A Lifetime

LIANA BROOKS

INKLET #065

Shoe

AMY LAURENS

INKLET #066

Published AUTHOR

LIANA BROOKS

DOUBLE ISSUE   INKLET #067

THE REMARKABLE INSIGHT OF JELLYBEANS & Understanding

AMY LAURENS

INKLET #068

Desperate Measures

AMY LAURENS

INKLET #069

Rock-a-bye

LIANA BROOKS

INKLET #070

the Other Carly

AMY LAURENS

INKLET #071

By Bioluminescent light

AMY LAURENS

INKLET #072

Even Villains Grant Wishes
A Heroes & Villains Story

LIANA BROOKS

Lightning Source UK Ltd.
Milton Keynes UK
UKHW010642100521
383461UK00002B/304